To my son, Jenks

You are always my inspiration.
My hope for all children
is that they be loved as you are.

Copyright ©1998 by The Junior League of Charleston, Inc.
Printed in the United States of America

Published and distributed by
The Junior League of Charleston, Inc.
51 Folly Road
Charleston, South Carolina 29407
(843) 763-5284   Fax (843) 763-1626

L. J. Thompson, writer, illustrator, layout designer

Edited and manufactured by
The Children's Marketplace, an imprint of FRP
2451 Atrium Way
Nashville, Tennessee 37214
1-800-358-0560

Ronald Kidd, Project Editor
Bruce Gore, Project Designer

Thompson, Laura Jenkins. 1955–
        Joseph's Charleston adventure / Laura Jenkins Thompson.
            p.   cm.
        Summary: While trying to help a lost puppy find her way home,
    Joseph visits the famous sights of Charleston, South Carolina.
        ISBN 0-9607854-1-8
        [1. Charleston (S.C.)—Fiction. 2. Dogs—Fiction.]   I. Junior
    League of Charleston (S.C.)   II. Title
    PZ7.T3716115Da1   1998
    [E]—dc21
                                              97-42833
                                                CIP
                                                AC

The artwork for each picture was prepared using watercolor and ink.

Joseph's Charleston Adventure

Written and Illustrated by

LAURA JENKINS THOMPSON

The Junior League of Charleston, Inc.
Charleston, South Carolina

Joseph loved playing on the wide sidewalk in front of his Charleston home. One sunny spring morning he was skipping along, spinning around the lampposts and whistling a cheery tune.

All of a sudden Joseph stopped whistling. He heard the sound of crying nearby. Under a tall palmetto tree, he saw a Boykin spaniel puppy huddled in a ball.

"What's wrong, little puppy?" asked Joseph in a kind voice.

To his surprise, the puppy answered.

"I'm lost," she whimpered. "I followed a pretty yellow butterfly out my garden gate and along some crooked streets. Now I can't find my way home."

"What's your name?" Joseph asked.

"Susie," she said. "That's short for Miss Suzannah Sarah Seabrook."

Joseph introduced himself and said, "Maybe we can retrace your steps, Susie. Where were you last?"

"I remember a park where children were climbing on cannons," sniffed the puppy. "There were cannonballs stacked like pyramids."

Joseph smiled and said, "Follow me."

Joseph led her down toward the water to a grassy park
shaded by live oaks.

"This is the place!" cried Susie. "I remember families having
picnics by the gazebo and the pigeons chasing after crumbs."

"It's called White Point Gardens, or the Battery," Joseph
said. "Most of the cannons are from the Civil War."

"What else can you remember?" asked Joseph.

Susie thought for a moment. "I remember seeing houses that were all painted different colors," she said.

"That sounds like East Bay Street," said Joseph. "Let's go take a look."

Joseph picked Susie up and walked along the High Battery seawall. Susie sniffed the salty ocean breeze and looked out onto the historic harbor that was dotted with sailboats and motorboats.

As they passed a row of stately mansions, an elderly lady waved to them from one of the wide piazzas facing the sea.

Soon, they reached a row of candy-colored houses across from a playground full of children. Two teenagers glided by on roller blades.

"These are the houses!" exclaimed Susie, wagging her tail. "I remember them painted different colors like jelly beans."

Joseph laughed and said, "This part of East Bay Street is called Rainbow Row. Let's walk up to the corner. Maybe you'll remember something else there."

At the corner stood the Old Exchange Building. Susie
peeked through the bars of the dungeon. Pirate Stede Bonnet
had been held prisoner on this site in 1718.

On the porch was a young man with a tricorn hat and knee
breeches like those worn during the American Revolution. He
was playing a tin whistle.

"I remember that tune!" cried Susie, leaping up and down
with excitement.

"Good afternoon," called the young man.
"What can I do for y'all today?"

"This little puppy is lost," replied Joseph. "Might you know
where she lives?"

"I saw her on Broad Street earlier," said the young man,
pointing down the wide old avenue. "Why don't you look there?"

Joseph and Susie scurried down Broad Street, past the law offices and the banks. Black signs with gold lettering announced each address, while old palmetto trees guarded the entrances. Overhead, the bells of St. Michael's Church chimed the hour.

The pair entered Washington Park, a shady spot next to City Hall. Joseph paused to drink at the old green fountain while Susie sniffed the flowers around the monuments. As the little chocolate-brown dog chased a squirrel up a tree, she spied a road paved with cobblestones.

"There's that bumpety road!" she cried. "I think I'm getting close to home!"

Joseph scooped up the puppy and hugged her tight. Then, holding her close, he walked on tiptoe across the bumpy cobblestones of Chalmers Street. They passed rows of single houses with lovely side gardens and the Pink House with its old tile roof.

Turning the corner at Church Street, Joseph sat down on the steps of the Dock Street Theatre to rest a moment. Susie wandered around the columns and strolled up toward the old west cemetery of St. Philip's Church.

"Peep, peep, peep!"

Susie stopped sniffing and looked around. Beside the old cemetery gate was a nest of Carolina wrens that had fallen to the ground. The baby birds were quivering with fright.

Forgetting her own worries, Susie ran back to get Joseph. When the two of them returned, they looked up and saw that the nest had fallen from a ledge on the steeple, beneath a row of carved angels.

"I think the birds want to go home," said Susie.

Joseph nodded. He gently picked up the nest and, holding Susie under one arm, began to climb the winding stairs of the steeple. Round and round he climbed, higher and higher.

When he reached the top, Joseph carefully placed the nest back where it belonged. As he did, the church bells began to chime.

From the steeple, Joseph and Susie could look out over the rooftops of Charleston. Red, green, gold, and silver tin roofs sparkled in the sunlight.

"I think I see my home!" exclaimed Susie.

Susie scrambled down the steeple steps and hurried off through the streets with Joseph close behind. As they passed through the Old City Market, the familiar scent of cooking shrimp, oysters, and scallops filled the air. The busy vendors called out to shoppers, and Susie answered with a happy bark.

"I'm almost home," she cried, wagging her tail joyfully.

Susie rounded Anson Square, where the basket ladies were weaving fresh sweetgrass, an art form that has been passed down from mother to daughter for generations.

"Hello, Susie," laughed one of the basket ladies. "Where have you been?"

Susie recognized the voice of her friend Louise. "Now I know where I am," she thought.

Joseph followed Susie past rows of carriages that were full of happy families. The horses seemed to wink as Susie ran by. Joseph could hardly keep up with the excited puppy as she rounded the corner.

There on tree-lined Hasell Street were rows of single houses
made of brick with earthquake bolts on their walls and fancy
ironwork around their gardens. One lacy gate with a polished
brass knob suddenly flew open.

Joseph and Susie found themselves surrounded by Boykin spaniels! Susie's mother and father and all her brothers and sisters licked and kissed and hugged and squished Susie and her new friend.

Joseph waved goodbye to the happy family. He turned the corner, pulling on the sweet honeysuckle that hung from the brick fences. As he passed the houses, he twirled the *S*-shaped shutter dogs by each window.

As the sun set, Joseph headed down the narrow, crooked streets of Charleston toward home. Skipping up the slate walk to his own front steps, Joseph greeted his mother at the door with a big hug and a grin.

Learn more about Charleston…

The **Boykin spaniel** is a chocolate-brown dog with curly hair. It is the state dog of South Carolina. This happy and energetic hunting dog is wonderful with children.

A **Carolina wren** is a small brown-and-yellow bird. It is the state bird of South Carolina.

Charleston, South Carolina, became a city in 1670, one hundred years before America became a country. The city was first named Charles Towne after England's King Charles II. Charleston and all of America were still part of England at the time.

The **Civil War**, or War Between the States, started in Charleston in 1861 when the first shots were fired on Fort Sumter. During this war, the Confederacy (southern states) fought the Union (northern states).

Cobblestones are large rocks which were brought over from Europe in ships. The ships used the stones as ballast, or weight, to make the bottom of the ships heavier when they were not carrying cargo. Later these stones were used to pave roads such as Chalmers Street.

The **Dock Street Theatre** is located on the site of one of the first playhouses in America. In 1735, there was a creek beside the theatre, and the street next to the theatre was named Dock Street. That same street is now Queen Street, but the creek is no longer there.

Earthquake bolts were first installed in Charleston houses after the earthquake of 1886. Builders placed metal rods through the floors and ceilings of the houses. The rods were pulled tight with large bolts at each end to make the damaged homes secure again.

The **Four Corners of Law** is the intersection of Broad and Meeting Streets. The name refers to the four types of law represented at each corner: city, state, federal, and God's law.

High Battery is a seawall which protects the city of Charleston from the Charleston Harbor. It is wide enough that several people can walk along the top of the wall at the same time.

Charleston is known for its wide assortment of **ironwork**. Many different iron patterns are used to decorate the gates and fences surrounding the beautiful gardens. Some patterns are lacy like snowflakes, while others form swords or arrows.

The **Old City Market** was founded shortly after the American Revolution. People have been buying goods in this open-air market in much the same way for over two hundred years.

Built by the British in 1771, the **Old Exchange Building** is located at the end of Broad Street. Many important events happened there. George Washington danced in the Great Hall upstairs, and the dungeon was used before and during the American Revolution.

The **old west cemetery** is a graveyard where many famous people have been buried, such as a signer of the Declaration of Independence and a vice-president of the United States. It has very interesting gravestones and monuments.

The **palmetto tree** is the state tree of South Carolina. It has a spongy trunk with wide leaves, called fronds, at the top. A picture of the palmetto tree is on the South Carolina state flag.

A **piazza** (pronounced pe-az'-a) is a type of wide porch with a high ceiling which is found on many Charleston homes. Piazzas are located along the side of the house to keep the hot sun out of the windows. They also provide a place to enjoy the cool ocean breezes.

The **Pink House** is one of the oldest buildings in Charleston. It has been painted pink since the early 1600s and has been through many hurricanes, fires, and even an earthquake.

Rainbow Row is a row of colorful houses, most of which are connected, along East Bay Street. They were built in the 1700s as merchants' houses. The stores were on the first floor, and the living quarters were above.

St. Michael's Episcopal Church, located at the Four Corners of Law, is the oldest surviving church building in Charleston. The steeple served as the city's lookout and alarm tower until the late 1800s, and the clock has been the city's timekeeper since 1764.

St. Philip's Episcopal Church, formed in 1680, is the oldest church congregation in the Southeast. The present church building was built in 1835 after the earlier church was destroyed by fire. The steeple has served as a lighthouse for ships, and the church bells were melted to form cannon during the Civil War.

Shutter dogs are decorative pieces of ironwork made into clasps to keep window shutters open. These are attached to the side of the house beside windows. Many shutter dogs are shaped to look like the letter *S*.

The **single house** is a style of home unique to Charleston. It is built only one room wide with piazzas on each floor. The long narrow houses are built sideways, with the short side on the street, to take advantage of the ocean breezes.

Sweetgrass baskets were made first by slaves who came from Africa. These baskets are woven from bulrush, palmetto fronds, pine needles, and sweetgrass. These are all grasses found in the marshes around Charleston.

Many of Charleston's old homes have **tin roofs**. Making the roof of metal prevented hot sparks coming out of chimneys from starting house fires. The tin roofs also helped prevent the spread of fires from one roof to another during the Civil War shellings.

Washington Park is a small park behind City Hall. The monument in the park was designed by Robert Mills, the architect of the Washington Monument. The park was named for the Washington Light Infantry, a group of soldiers who protected Charleston in its early years.

White Point Gardens overlooks the Charleston Harbor and was named for the oyster shells once found there. Fort Sumter is located in the harbor where the Ashley and Cooper rivers meet and can be seen from the southern tip of the park.

THE JUNIOR LEAGUE OF CHARLESTON, INC., is a nonprofit women's organization founded in 1923 to promote voluntarism and meet growing needs in the community. In affiliation with The Association of Junior Leagues International, Inc., the Charleston League seeks to focus its efforts and resources on identifying critical community needs, implementing innovative programs that serve as catalysts for community change, and leaving a legacy of empowered and trained volunteers who reflect the community's diverse cultural heritage. Major projects begun by The Junior League of Charleston, Inc., include the Charleston Speech and Hearing Center, Horizon House, Saturday Soup Kitchen, and the Lowcountry Children's Center. Today, over 1,300 members from varied ethnic and religious backgrounds work throughout the greater Charleston area creating financial, volunteer, and advocacy resources to support League projects, as well as programs in partnership with other community groups. Proceeds from the sale of this book will help to further this work.

The Junior League of Charleston, Inc., would like to give special thanks to

- sustaining member of the Charleston League, Laura Jenkins Thompson, for her countless hours spent in writing and illustrating this book and for her most generous gift in donating this book so that the League can further its causes. Many individuals have contributed their time and talents to this project, but it would not be a reality without Laura;

- project editor Ronald Kidd and the entire staff of FRP for their expertise and guidance in editing and planning this book;

- the many community leaders and friends of the League for their help and advice in the initial phases of developing this fundraiser;

- and the numerous Junior League members for their work in developing, planning, researching, editing, and marketing this project. The vision, enthusiasm, and dedication of these women will be evidenced in programs throughout the Charleston area for many years to come.

LAURA JENKINS THOMPSON is a native Charlestonian and an award-winning designer, author, and teacher. She has a B.A. in Fine Arts and an M.Ed. in Special Education and has been teaching Charleston youths for over eighteen years. Mrs. Thompson also travels throughout the country teaching needlework. Her popular articles, patterns, and designs, as well as a best-selling book, have led her to be an internationally recognized needlearts expert. Many of her designs are showcased at her shop, Laura's Closet, in historic Charleston. Voluntarism always has played an important role in Mrs. Thompson's life. She has served on the boards of numerous national and local nonprofit organizations and continues to serve her community in a variety of ways. Laura still finds time in her busy schedule for her husband of twenty years, Joe, and her teenage son, Jenks, whose younger image serves as the model for Joseph in this book.

Mrs. Thompson would like to give special thanks to

- my husband, Joe Thompson, for all his love, for his continual support, and for his encouragement for over twenty years;

- my son, Jenks Thompson, for all the joy that he continues to bring to me daily;

- my parents, Lois and Midge Jenkins, for their love, for fostering my creativity at an early age, and for always being there;

- my wonderful friends and colleagues at Mason Preparatory School for their help, advice, and support throughout the writing and illustrating process;

- my delightful students at Mason Preparatory School for help that only children can give;

- my friends in the Junior League of Charleston for their encouragement and belief in me;

- and Snookie, for her doggie images.